Alex and Ace
The Adventure of the Purple Pendant

Written by

Susan Steinman

Alex and Ace: The Adventure of the Purple Pendant
Published through: IngramSpark

This is a work of fiction. Names, characters, places, and incidents are the product of the author's imagination or are used fictitiously. Any resemblance to actual persons, living or dead, events, or locales is entirely coincidental.

ISBN: 978-0-578-96821-6 (Paperback Edition)

For Kaylin, Kason, and Nolan.

*May endless love and the swirl of magic
surround you every day.*

CHAPTER 1

Starry Night

"The stars are mansions built by Nature's hand..."
~William Wordsworth

A dark shape swooped over Alex's head, visible against the glowing red embers in the fire pit. She looked up with a start as a large black crow landed on a nearby branch. Her best friend, Ace, giggled as the bird watched them.

"Where did you come from, buddy?" he asked.

Alex shook her head and went back to turning the stick slowly, with the marshmallow secured. "It looks perfect," she said with a sigh. The sides were evenly browned.

"Nice, Alex. Are you ready?"

Alex nodded as Ace handed her two crackers and a piece of chocolate. Alex carefully slid the marshmallow off the stick between the crackers and chocolate. She smooshed it together and, as the chocolate began to melt, she took a big bite. Ace smiled at her as he prepared to toast his next marshmallow.

He chuckled. "I think I'll have one more." The crow gave them one more quizzical look and flew away. Alex and Ace looked at each other.

"I guess he didn't want any," Alex said with a smile.

Alex's dog, Rocky, a good tempered three-year-old labradoodle, looked up at her expectantly, wondering if he was going to be able to share the treat. "No, boy," Alex said gently. "You can't have chocolate…it would make you sick."

Rocky lobbed a hopeful look at Ace and then went over, circled around on his blanket several times, and plopped down.

Alex enjoyed her treat. She looked up at the dark sky. There was a small sliver of the moon visible. The Milky Way cut a swath of silvery mystery across the sky, billions of stars strong. Alex felt peaceful and content.

"Ace…look, there is another satellite!"

"Oh yes. Good spotting…look how fast it's going." The satellite was high and moving north to south. It looked like a star but was moving quickly. They had been watching satellites all night. Her dad told her that the sky was filled with them, crisscrossing on their journey above Earth. Alex imagined what it might be like to sit on top of one.

If I knew I couldn't fall off, and I was safe… she thought, imagining herself soaring above the mountains, looking down at the rivers and lakes. *It would be so cool.*

Alex Elsy Emerson and Ace Howard Keats were both eleven years old. They were camping up in the high country, in Sweetwater Canyon in the Rocky Mountains of Colorado. Home was about an hour and a half away in a small town called Aspen Acres, located in the southwest part of the state, close to the Sangre de Cristo Mountain range.

They were with their dads, who were sitting close by talking quietly and laughing.

Alex's dad was a geologist and studied rocks. Alex thought her dad was the smartest and most fun person ever. Ace's dad was fun to be around, too, Alex thought. Ace said his dad worked from home and knew all about computers.

The kids finished the treats. "Now I'm ready for sleep. My belly is full," Ace said with a smile.

Alex was feeling sleepy, too, and was ready to crawl into her sleeping bag. "Good night, Ace. We are going to have so much fun tomorrow."

Ace nodded in agreement.

Mr. Keats got up. "Let's get you settled into our tent, son."

Mr. Emerson came over. "C'mon, honey. Let's get you tucked in." He unzipped the flap to the tent. The air was chilly, so Alex snuggled into her sleeping bag. Rocky came in. He liked to sleep close to her feet. Alex could feel the warmth of her canine friend wrap around her toes.

"Good night, Dad…." She sighed. She loved camping with her dad. It was even more fun with Ace and his dad, she thought.

He placed a kiss on her forehead. "Good night, sweetheart. I'm going to tend to the fire and make sure it is out. See you in the morning. We are going to get up early and go panning. I'm super grateful you came with me. It's going to be fun." He smiled, tousled her head, and zipped the tent flap shut.

The Emerson family had a nighttime ritual of sharing one thing they were grateful for. Alex was excited about panning. She wondered what they might find. Alex thought for a moment. She was grateful for her warm sleeping bag, she decided. She was grateful that she had met Ace a few months before, when his family moved down the street from them. She was grateful for the beautiful fox they saw when they were hiking before dinner. The fox stopped for a second and looked at them before scampering away. Alex loved nature. So many beautiful things to see, she thought.

She missed her mom, who was away at work. She was in Costa Rica, taking photographs of volcanos for a magazine. Alex closed her eyes and imagined her mom's arms around her, giving her a good night hug. She sent her mom a warm hug back and hoped she could feel it. She nestled a little bit deeper into the downy comfort and, feeling quite content, Alex drifted off to sleep.

CHAPTER 2

Panning Adventure

"Do not follow where the path may lead.
Go instead where there is no path and leave a trail."
~Ralph Waldo Emerson

Alex woke up early. The sun was just starting to come up over the eastern horizon, the dimmer switch slowing turning up, brightening the day and warming the ground. Her dad was sleeping. Alex quietly unzipped the flap to the tent, and she and Rocky went outside. Rocky scampered away and started sniffing around the pine trees. Alex heard the other tent flap being unzipped.

Ace came out yawning. "Morning, Alex," he said. "Let's eat!"

The kids went to the car, where they had stowed their cooler and food. They kept it away from the camp and tent because they did not want to attract bears or other animals.

Alex looked around to make sure there were no furry creatures visiting. She pulled out cereal, milk, and ripe peaches from the cooler and brought them over to the picnic table. Ace grabbed blueberry muffins. Mr. Emerson came out of the tent, yawning. He smiled when he saw that breakfast was ready. He started the camp stove to boil water for coffee for the adults and hot chocolate for the kids.

Mr. Keats soon joined them. "Morning, everyone," he said, as Mr. Emerson handed him a cup of coffee. "And breakfast is ready? This fresh air is making me very hungry. Thank you."

Alex smiled when she thought about how eager Ace and his dad were to eat. She poured two scoops of dog nuggets into Rocky's bowl, and he happily started chomping.

Alex's dad said a morning blessing, and they all dove into their camp breakfast. "Good stuff," her dad said happily.

"Yep," Alex responded, full and content. Her hot chocolate tasted good out of a camp tin cup, she thought, as she took her final sip.

"Okay, kids, ready to go panning?" Mr. Keats asked.

Alex was excited. She and her dad had been prospecting a few times over the summer. They had discovered some pretty rocks, but Alex was hopeful they would find gold nuggets today. After breakfast was over, the kids cleaned up the table.

"Okay, let's get the pans...and the strainer, and the shovels. Alex, grab the container we keep the dark dirt and gold dust in, too," Mr. Emerson said.

Alex helped get everything ready.

Ace said, "I'll pack the snacks." He gathered some apples and pretzels and refilled their water bottles from the big jug of spring water they'd brought. *I don't want to forget Rocky's treats,* he thought. He grabbed the box of dog biscuits and put a handful into a baggie. Ace loved Rocky. He hoped his mom would let him get a dog someday.

They started down the path. Mr. Emerson said they were at about 8,000 feet. They walked through an aspen grove. The tall, thin, stately trees were beautiful, Alex thought. The leaves from the trees were a rich, beautiful green, twinkling softly in the gentle morning breeze. It was cool in the shade, but the sun was rising quickly, and the patches of warmth were expanding.

They came to a small stream. It was protected by a four-foot rock wall on the north side. Mr. Emerson scratched at the wall. "Here we go, guys. Let's try here. See how the dirt is black close to the rock? That means there might be minerals in it."

The stream was shallow but had a good flow of water. It was a tributary of the Arkansas River, which began far up in the mountains near Leadville and flowed all the way to the Mississippi.

Alex's dad dug a shovel full of rich, dark soil from the rock and put it in a pan. He swirled the pan in the water, washing out the lighter dirt as the heavier dark dirt settled into the bottom and sides. Alex and Ace each had a smaller pan and followed his lead. As the lighter dirt and rocks washed away, dark soil with glints of gold remained. Mr. Keats helped as they carefully spooned this into a jar to take home and separate later. They continued this process several times.

Alex said, "Ace, do you want to take a break? Let's go explore."

"Yes," Ace replied.

Ace and Alex ran by the bank of the stream, hopping from rock to rock when they could. Rocky was in the lead. He loved the cool water and was splashing and prancing. The shade from the trees offered respite from the warm sun.

Alex said, "Let's hang out here and watch the water." The water flowed over a larger rock, causing a small waterfall dumping into a protected basin. The sound of the falling water was peaceful.

Alex found a rock to sit on. Ace sat on a rock close by. "Hey, Ace, my mom would say this is a perfect place to meditate. Want to try?"

Ace shrugged his shoulders. "Sure, why not?"

"It's easy," Alex said. "Just focus on your breath. My mom taught me how to do this."

"Breathe in, one, two, three…breathe out, one, two, three." Alex felt relaxed and happy. Ace looked content, too. He had his eyes closed.

The sun was warm on her face. She watched the water bubbling over the rocks and wondered if any of the small stones would make their way all the way to the Mississippi River. What an adventure that would be, she thought.

A loud caw filled the air. Alex looked up at the tree branch above her. A crow was sitting on the branch watching them. Ace opened his eyes and looked up, too.

"I wonder if it's the same crow we saw last night?" Ace asked.

The bird was totally black except for a white mark on his chest. "Maybe he wants to meditate, too," he said. "He sure likes watching us." The kids giggled.

"He looks different than your average crow with that white spot," Alex said.

Ace agreed. The spot looked like a slightly irregular diamond.

The kids closed their eyes again. Alex tried to focus on her breath, but she kept thinking about the crow.

Rocky started to bark. He was digging by a tree close to the stream.

"What's up, boy?" Alex asked.

Ace opened his eyes and looked at the dog. "What's going on, Rocky?" Ace said.

Alex went over to where Rocky was sitting, looking into the hole he dug and quietly whining. "What did you find?" Alex dug into the dirt a little. "I don't think there is anything here." Alex looked up as the crow flew by and landed on the branch closer to them.

Ace joined her and dug in the hole. "I don't see anything," he said. "C'mon, Rocky, let's go explore more."

Rocky wouldn't move. Alex went back to the hole and used a flat rock to scoop out mud. She looked down. There was a purplish glow deep in the soil. "Ace, what is that?" she said.

Ace came over and peered down. "Whoa…" he said, "something in there is purple. It looks like a light."

Alex dug deeper. Suddenly, her fingers felt something hard. She tapped her fingers around the outline, a square shape. The dirt was heavy, but Alex and Ace scooped the wet mud from around it bit by bit. Finally, she pulled out a tin box.

"Wow," Ace said. Rocky cocked his head to one side and then scampered down to the stream. Ace said, "Good idea. Let's wash it off."

Alex and Ace went down to the stream and swished water around the box. It was about 6 inches tall and 7 inches long. It was rusty, but they could make out letters on the top. The dirt washed off, and she turned it over. She heard something clank inside. "There's something in it, Ace...." Alex tried to pry the top open. It was stuck.

Ace attempted to open it, too. "Let's try this flat rock," he said.

The kids worked together, tapping along the edges of the box. They rinsed it again and kept tapping. Finally, the top opened with a final tug. Alex's heart was beating fast as she looked inside. There was a chain with a pendant embedded with stones.

"How odd," she said to Ace. "It's got a purple glow around it."

She handed the box to Ace, who whistled under his breath. "Wow." The glow faded and disappeared.

Alex pulled the pendant out of the box, and they gently washed it in the water. There was a large purple stone embedded in the middle of the pendant, surrounded by small red stones. The kids looked at each other. They heard a loud caw and looked up at the crow, who was still watching them. The crow seemed to nod his head and opened his beak again. Then he swooped down slightly, flying by the kids, and disappeared from sight.

Alex put the pendant and chain in the box and lightly closed the lid. The box felt warm in her hand. "Ace, let's go show our dads."

"C'mon, Rocky," Ace said. Rocky scampered ahead of them as the kids ran back.

Their dads were sitting on a tree log, eating apples.

"Dad! Look what we found!" Alex rushed over.

"What do you have, hon?" Her dad picked up the box. "Wow, guys...this is really old." He carefully examined the tin box. "I think it's a tea box. See these letters? I bet it's over one hundred years old."

"Look inside, Dad.... There's a necklace in there!"

Mr. Emerson opened the box and gently took it out.

"Wow...this is cool. This is an unusual chain, and just look at that gorgeous amethyst."

He handed it to Ace's dad to look at. The chain was heavy, about twenty inches long. The pendant was attached to the chain. It was diamond-shaped, and the amethyst was embedded within. The amethyst was surrounded by small red stones. Mr. Keats said, "I think those might be rubies. Well, kids, that is quite a find! I bet this pendant is old as well."

They took it over to the water, and Mr. Emerson washed more dirt and mud off it, then gently dried it with a cloth.

"Well, kids, I think you found a beautiful piece of jewelry," he said, sounding thoughtful. "I wonder how it ended up here."

Alex and Ace were wondering the same thing. "Can we keep it?"

"I think so. There's no way to identify where it came from or how long it's been here. This is going to be a nice souvenir."

Alex said, "Yes, we can share it, Ace. Do you want to keep it first?"

Ace smiled. "Thanks, but you keep it. It's a necklace, and I think it will look better on you." They all laughed.

Alex gave her friend a hug. "Thank you! You can borrow it whenever you want!"

Alex smiled as she put the pendant and chain back in the box and wrapped it up in a cloth her dad gave her. She tucked it into her backpack.

The morning passed quickly. They found several pink quartz stones. Ace washed several in the stream. "My mom will love these," he said.

Alex agreed. "Yes, they are so pretty."

They washed out the panning supplies, and Mr. Emerson put them in his knapsack. The group headed back to camp for lunch.

CHAPTER 3

Saturday Slide

"It's not what you look at that matters, it's what you see."
~Henry David Thoreau

The sun was warm, and a few wispy clouds floated by. Several hammocks hung between pine trees, and the dads were stretched out resting.

Alex had the pendant in her hand. It felt warm. Ace said, "Hey, let's go back to the stream and look around some more." Alex agreed.

Mr. Emerson said, "Okay, kids, but take Rocky with you."

Rocky eagerly got up from his nap and looked at the kids with a happy expression.

The three of them followed the path through the aspen grove and soon arrived at the stream. They walked to the area where they had found the pendant. There was a large, flat stone by the stream, and they sat down. Alex handed the pendant to Ace. "It's so warm," she said.

Ace held it. "Yes, and it almost looks like that glow is back," he said thoughtfully.

They looked up at the tree limb above them. The crow was sitting there. He swooped down and landed on the far end of the rock they were sitting on and looked at them. His eyes looked kind, Alex thought.

The bird nodded several times at them, and then hopped to another rock closer to the aspen grove. He looked at them and nodded again.

Ace said, "I think he wants us to follow him."

Alex replied, "Well, okay, as long as we don't go too far."

The bird continued to hop from rock to rock, flapping his wings. They came to a clearing in the trees. There was a large, flat rock face jutting out from the hill. It was smooth. There was a fallen tree making a perfect spot for the kids to sit down. Rocky looked around, circled around several times on a bed of leaves before lying down, and then closed his eyes. Alex looked at Ace. "Well, I guess it's okay because Rocky seems pretty comfortable."

The bird was now on a branch about six feet up from the ground. He continued to watch the kids carefully. He nodded at the kids and then used his beak to knock against a knob on the tree. He did it three times. The pendant remained warm, and the faint purple glow grew quicky in front of them, forming an oblong shape that appeared like a door. Alex was shocked, and her eyes widened as the shape grew clearer. "Ace, what is that?" she whispered.

Ace shook his head. "I'm not sure, but I think the bird wants us to go through it."

The crow was standing by the shape now and continued to nod his head. Alex looked at him and saw that his beak was curved up in a smile. The haze grew larger, and then the kids saw a door appear in the middle. They heard a low, deep voice.

"Welcome." The door opened slightly.

Ace looked at Alex again, puzzled. Then Ace shrugged his shoulders. "Okay, let's go." He stuck his right foot into the haze where the door was. Suddenly, he disappeared into the mist. Alex was scared but stuck her foot in, too. Suddenly, she was pulled in. She could hear Ace talking to her and the caw of a crow but could see nothing. She was moving very fast, like she was gliding down a slippery, curvy slide. Her heart was beating fast.

Suddenly, she landed on the ground with a gentle thud. She looked around. Ace was standing next to her. The haze was gone, but the pendant still felt warm in her hand.

"What was that, Ace?" she asked in amazement.

Ace shook his head. "I have no idea. But the coolest thing ever?"

Alex looked around. "And where are we?"

They were standing on the top of a green hill with gentle slopes. There was a large, flat rock by several aspen trees. To the west, Alex saw a large swath of mountains. Several towered over the others. One had jagged edges jutting up to the top. There was a valley.

Alex was confused. She said, "That one looks like Crestone. How can that be? Nothing else looks familiar."

When Alex saw Crestone from the hill close by her house, she could also see the downtown area of Aspen Acres, the lights from the street, and the tall courthouse with a giant clock on it.

This view looked the same, but there was nothing in the valley but a meadow and several cabins.

She continued. "It looks the same, but there is no town there."

Ace was thoughtful. "Yes, that is really strange. Where's the courthouse? We can see that from the hill at the end of our road."

There was an aspen grove on the side of the hill that opened into a green meadow. Cows were in the pasture, munching on grass. They were unconcerned by the presence of the kids. The cabin closest to the bottom of the hill looked inviting. There were several shade trees and big pots of flowers placed across the yard and on the porch. There were cheery yellow curtains hung in the windows. A young woman came out the door. She had flowing red hair and a kind smile. There were chickens running around the yard, and the kids could see her throwing seeds on the ground, which the birds eagerly pecked at.

Ace looked up at the aspen tree closest to the rock. The black crow was sitting on the branch, the same white diamond shape on its chest. He nudged Alex and pointed. "Look!"

"About time you got here," the crow said. "Your trip wasn't too bad, I hope?" he said, with a quizzical look.

13

Alex and Ace's mouth dropped open in astonishment.

The crow continued. "We've been waiting a long time."

The bird flew off the branch and landed on the ground several feet from the kids.

Alex leaned back.

"Don't worry," the bird said. "I mean no harm. I'm here to help you both."

The crow's eyes softened, and Alex saw his beak turn up in a smile.

"How can you talk?" Alex managed to sputter out.

"Many things you think are impossible are completely common here. I am Corvus Merle Raven," he said proudly, as the feathers on his chest ruffled. The bird bowed. "Delighted to make your acquaintance."

Ace's eyes widened, and he shook his head. "Happy to meet you, too."

Alex nodded in agreement, although she felt like she was in a dream. The bird nodded back.

Alex and Ace looked at each other.

Alex said with wonder, "Corvus, where are we?"

Corvus shook his feathers and cocked his head.

"You are in Aspen Acres, Colorado!"

Ace quietly said, "But we live in Aspen Acres, and this looks nothing like it. And we were camping up in Sweetwater Canyon. How did we get here?"

"Well, not everything is as it seems," the bird chirped. "It's exactly the same and totally different," he continued. "You are in a magical place. A powerful place." He looked thoughtful. "You might say it is retro here."

Alex was astonished.

"Magic has always been a part of this world. It's as normal as the sun rising and the sun setting. Magic keeps everything moving forward as it should. It helps guide us to do things that we like. We may not see it, but it's there. It can cause a bird like me to talk." Corvus thrust his head up proudly. "It can even influence a camping trip so that two good friends will find a pendant and know it is special."

Alex's eyes widened again. She looked at Ace with a look of wonderment.

"Corvus," Alex said, "we saw you watching us."

Corvus looked at her kindly. "Yes, that was me." Corvus continued to explain. "Some people call magic a coincidence. I happen to know it is a well-orchestrated series of events that happen for the good. Magic is intertwined, just like the aspen grove we see whose roots support each other under the surface. The pendant was lost a long time ago. It has powers you will soon experience. You two are the only ones to see and experience that in the 'normal' world. The only other human who can see it is its rightful owner. And that is who we need to find. You both have the power to do so. I'm here to help protect and guide you as I can, but it rests in your hands."

"You brought us here?" Alex asked.

"Absolutely! I knew you were both ready, and you are obviously quite clever and brave."

Alex and Ace sat down on the rock and continued to listen.

"Why us?" Ace asked.

Alex added, "And what are you protecting us from?"

Corvus explained. "You have been chosen by the Council of All Good Everywhere. We are known as CAGE. They knew exactly what to do to set up the events that you were a part of."

Ace and Alex let that information sink in.

"There is a balance in the world. Right now, there is more good magic than bad. But it's getting close to tipping the other way. When the pendant was lost, we had fifty years to find it again and reunite it with its owner. If that is not done by the deadline, the magic in the pendant stops forever.

"The pendant is infused with good magic and was created by a powerful man. He knew how to talk to the animal kingdom. It was the greatest partnership ever, and they worked together to create the healing powers within it. He wanted to hide the magic in a place where it would stay safely hidden. He gave it to his wife, who was a very powerful healer. The pendant absorbed his creative powers and her healing abilities. She passed it down to her daughter, Maddie Longfellow. Maddie lives in that cabin by the trees." Corvus pointed to the cabin where they had seen the woman with the long red hair. "That is what you have in your hand now, Alex."

Alex looked at the pendant, and her eyes widened more.

"The magic is still strong, but time is of the essence. We have exactly six days, ten hours, and thirty minutes to get this pendant to Maddie." Corvus looked up. "Let's see, today is Saturday. We must reunite her with the pendant by next Friday before midnight. You are seeing Maddie as she was fifty years ago. Your mission is to get the pendant back to her." His voice was urgent.

"How do we find her?" Alex asked.

Corvus shook his head sadly. "We do not know. When she lost the pendant, the magic went on hold. We have no way of knowing where she is. We think she remained in the area, but once the pendant was lost, our connection to her whereabouts ended." Corvus continued. "CAGE noticed you both in the area and some mild pings were sent out by the pendant."

Alex said, "Rocky found it! He started digging, and we knew it was something."

Ace added, "Yes, and then we saw the purple glow in the mud and water."

Corvus looked pleased. "Rocky did very well. Dogs have excellent hearing, and he must have been following the sound. We know you two can do it. Otherwise, the Council of All Good Everywhere— otherwise known as CAGE—would never have chosen you."

Corvus ruffled his feathers and cocked his beak. He looked intent as he said, "Alex, you asked what we are protecting you from. There are some who want the magic to go away forever."

Alex and Ace were mesmerized.

"There was another powerful man. He created an amulet. However, this amulet was infused with greed. His family used the amulet for No Good. He used it so his crop was bountiful, but also so that other crops in his community failed. Rain would fall over his farm, and it would be dry and dusty on a neighboring farm. This way he could glean all the profits. The animals in the area became aware something was amiss, and CAGE was formed to battle bad magic and support the growth of good. After a great battle, CAGE was able to obtain this amulet and stop the family from creating No Good. They were very angry about that and set their sights on trying to take Maddie's pendant in hopes of turning its magic to suit their own needs."

Corvus was interrupted by the sound of a dog barking. Alex looked down the hill at a cabin in the distance. A dog was sitting by the front door. A man walked out the door. "Stop barking!" he yelled. He looked around, as if to see whether anyone was around. "It's fine. Stop it."

Corvus said urgently, "Come here, kids. Get under this tree. I don't want him to see you."

The kids scampered to the aspen tree. Corvus hopped up on a branch and whispered.

The tree trunk bent over to cast a shadow of leaves and protection over the kids. There was enough shade so that no one would be able to see them.

Ace and Alex's eyes widened. Corvus saw the look of disbelief on their faces. "Don't worry. You will get used to it. Remember, here, magic is everywhere."

The children watched as the man and dog got into an old red pickup truck. The engine of the truck sputtered a few times before it started. The man looked annoyed, and seemed to be yelling, but the kids could not hear what he was saying. Finally, the car engine started. The man drove down a long driveway, and the truck turned down the road.

"Thank you, my friend," Corvus whispered to the tree.

The leaves rippled in the breeze. "No problem," the voice from the tree responded.

As the truck disappeared, the tree trunk straightened out.

"Thank you," Alex whispered. The leaves swayed in the breeze again. Alex was sure she heard the tree respond, "You are welcome. That's what I'm here for."

Ace touched the trunk with wonder and shook his head.

"Corvus, who is that?" Alex asked. "Why don't you want him to see us?"

The bird hopped onto the rock and sighed heavily. "He is the one who wants to steal the magic forever. His name is Rusty Stone Heart. It was his family that used the other amulet for greed." Corvus shook his head.

"If he knew you had the pendant, he would do whatever he could to take it. He would try to infuse it with Greed and No Good, and then he would have his power restored. If we can reunite the pendant with Maddie now, Rusty will be powerless."

Alex was intrigued. "Corvus, why is the pendant warm when we touch it?"

Corvus answered, "You are feeling the energy within it. It feels warm to you and Ace, but likely would not for anyone else. You two are connected to it."

Ace nodded. "That makes sense. My dad didn't notice it being warm."

Alex looked thoughtful. *I can't wait to talk to Ace,* she thought. She felt panicked. "How are we going to get back to camp?"

At the same time, Ace blurted out, "Corvus, how do we get back? My dad is going to be worried."

Alex agreed. "I think we've been gone a long time," she said.

Corvus hopped close by them. "No worries," he said. "Let's get you back now. Time is different here. You've only been gone about ten minutes. One thing I want you kids to remember. Don't show the pendant to anyone except your parents. It could be big trouble if it gets into the wrong hands."

"Okay," Alex said a bit nervously.

"This is what I want you to do. Go home and rest. Talk this over with each other. If you decide you want to help, go to your treehouse tomorrow afternoon. I'll be around, and we can talk more."

Ace had a curious look. "How do you know I have a treehouse?"

Corvus looked at him with a smile. "I'm pretty sure I've been there before, but I'll save that story for another time." Corvus gave instructions. "Kids, stay on the rock. Hold the pendant together."

Alex closed her eyes. Ace put his hand over hers, so he was touching the pendant as well.

Corvus flew back up to the tree and tapped his beak three times on a knob sticking out. The purple haze came up quickly from the pendant and settled around the bottom of the rock. Within seconds, it grew, and soon the outline of a door appeared in the middle. They looked at Corvus. He nodded. "Go in."

Alex was scared, but calm. "We did this before," she said to Ace.

Ace replied with confidence, "Corvus knows what he is doing."

Alex put her hand in the haze and pushed on the door. She stuck her foot in. Ace did the same. The kids felt themselves being pulled in and moving very fast in the haze, like they were going down a slippery tubular slide. Less than a minute later, Alex felt her feet touch the ground. Rocky looked up at them with sleepy eyes.

"Well, boy, I guess you didn't miss us," Ace said.

Alex smiled and said, "We'd better get back to camp."

The kids arrived back to find their dads taking down the tent. "Hi guys," Mr. Emerson said. "You weren't gone too long. Did you kids find anything else?"

"Nothing but a talking crow," Ace said with a grin.

His dad looked at him and tousled his head. "That's my boy. You have such a great imagination."

Alex wanted to tell her dad about Corvus, but she knew she should not.

"Ready to go home, kids? We'll be home before dark. Alex, Mom should be home."

Alex could tell Dad was excited Mom was coming home. Alex was glad, too.

They packed the jeep. Alex took a careful look around the campsite to make sure they were leaving it as nice as they'd found it. She found one of Rocky's toy bones and put it in the backseat.

"Okay, let's go home! Treasures intact! Forest creatures safe. Beautiful birds, lovely views," her dad said cheerfully. Seatbelts secured, they started down the mountain towards home.

Ace and Alex were talking quietly in the back seat. Rocky lay between them, and Alex was petting him. Ace was thoughtful. "This all seems crazy, but I want to help. If we can figure out who the pendant belongs to, we can help save magic."

"I want to do it, too," Alex agreed. "I never thought I would say this about a bird, but I trust Corvus. I'm not sure where we will start, but I want to go back to see him tomorrow."

Ace patted her hand. "We will figure it out," he said confidently.

Alex smiled. Ace was so brave, she thought. "My mom says when I have a problem I am trying to find a solution to, I can always go to them, or I can sleep on it. Sometimes when I wake up, I have figured out an idea."

"Okay," Ace said confidently. "Let's do it and see what tomorrow brings."

CHAPTER 4

Sunday Spells

"Nothing ever becomes real 'til it is experienced."
~ John Keats

Alex woke up early and flew out of bed full of energy. Mom always suggested she spend a few minutes before she got out of bed doing mindful breathing and thinking about what she was grateful for, but Alex was distracted. The rays from the sunrise were teasing the eastern horizon with a fair shake of expectation for a beautiful summer day.

Mom was making coffee. She gave Alex a hug. "Hi, honey. Are you ready for your day with Ace?" she asked. Dad gave her a hug as he sat reading the paper.

"Oh yes," she replied. "How long do I get to stay?"

"I'll drop you off after breakfast," he said, "and pick you up after dinner."

Alex was happy. She had a quick breakfast and ran upstairs to pack her backpack. She tucked the pendant in a pocket and closed the zipper. She ran back downstairs. "Mom, look at what I found yesterday." Alex showed her the pendant. "Dad said it is really old."

"Gosh, Alex, that is so pretty! It does look old. I love it! Look at those pretty stones."

Alex gave her mom a big hug. "I'm glad you're home, Mom."

Since her mom and dad were going to be gone most of the day, the Keats family had invited Alex to bring Rocky. "You have to be a good boy, Rocky," Alex whispered. Rocky sat up and looked at Alex, his tongue hanging out happily. She could have sworn he was smiling.

They decided to ride their bikes over. Rocky ran along, stopping once in a while to sniff a bush.

The road was windy but mostly flat. There were few houses on the road and little traffic. Limber pines and big-toothed maple trees lined the road, providing a peaceful, woody area for the creatures who lived there. Alex caught a whiff of a buttery vanilla scent and admired a huge, forest green Ponderosa pine. She watched a black squirrel scamper across the road and dart under the tree.

Her dad told her these were called Abert's squirrels. They were odd-looking but cute, Alex thought, noting the little black tuft of hair sticking up from its tiny head.

Ace and Mrs. Keats came out to welcome them. "Welcome, Alex," she said with a friendly voice. "Thanks for spending the day with us!"

Alex was glad for the warm greeting. Sometimes she felt nervous when she was away from her mom and dad.

Rocky made himself right at home by lapping up water from a dog bowl that was on the porch. He then circled around a dog bed. Mr. Emerson chuckled. "He is so spoiled! Thank you so much for watching him, too."

"No problem," Mrs. Keats said. "It will be great for Ace to have some company. We still have a lot of unpacking to do." She sighed as she looked behind her. Stacks of boxes filled the living room. "This is going to take a while, I'm afraid."

Mr. Emerson nodded his head. "It does take a while, but it will get done." He gave Alex a hug and got back on his bike. "See you later. Call if you need anything."

The kids and Mrs. Keats waved good-bye.

"Alex, do you want to go up in the treehouse?" Ace asked.

Alex was excited. Not only was Corvus going to meet them there, but Ace had the best treehouse in the entire world, she thought.

Mrs. Keats nodded. "Great idea, Ace. You know, Alex, my aunt had that built when I was a young girl. I used to come and stay with her in the summers. I love it up there."

She continued. "Ace's dad checked it all out when we moved here, and it is completely solid. It might need some dusting!"

"How wonderful," Alex said. "Your aunt must have been so nice."

They walked to the back yard. There were two large spruce trees, and the treehouse was nestled in the middle. There was a ladder firmly attached to the side of one of the trees. The sides of the ladder were birch limbs woven together to provide a strong hand hold. It was about thirteen feet off the ground.

They climbed up to a deck that circled the treehouse. The deck railing was woven together from the top of the rail to the bottom with thin branches also. It looked pretty, Alex thought. The deck was wide enough for several chairs to sit side by side. Alex looked around. It was so beautiful. There was a large basket sitting next to an opening in the rail connected by a pulley from the rail to the ground.

"Mom," Ace called out. "Can you send us up some cookies?"

He dropped the basket over and carefully lowered the chain until the basket reached the ground. Mrs. Keats smiled as she grabbed the basket. "You read my mind," she answered. "I'll be right back."

Ace opened the door. "C'mon in," he said cheerily.

Alex smiled when she got inside. It was cozy. A large, shaggy blue rug was in the middle of the floor. There was a large window to the west side that was opened slightly. Several throw blankets were neatly folded on the end of the bench. There was a basket to the side, filled with books and magazines. One wall had a large bench with a thick orange cushion and pillows to lean against. There was another ladder, which led up to a loft. Alex said, "Can we go up to the loft? It's so cool up there."

"Sure," Ace said. "We'll wait until Mom has the snacks ready, and we will take them up there."

Several family pictures were in frames. Alex looked over at a picture of a bird in a frame. "That's cool," she said, as she looked at a handwritten inscription on the frame. It was a picture of a crow sitting on a branch with a quizzical look. The wording under it was, "If you see the crow, you must go."

Ace said, "We found that in my aunt's stuff. I thought it was pretty cool, too, and Mom said I could keep it up here."

Alex looked at Ace. "You know who this looks like?" she said with a smile.

Ace replied, "I know. I was thinking about that last night. And Corvus said he would meet us here. I wonder if my aunt knew him?"

Alex said, "We will have to find out. That would be the coolest thing ever."

She plopped down on the cushion. "This is so comfortable," she said. "I love it!"

Ace agreed. "I can keep my stuff in the drawers underneath," he said with a smile. "And there are lights up here!" He pushed a light switch, and a gentle light filled the room.

"It's just perfect," Alex said.

"Thanks, Alex. I'm glad you like it," Ace replied.

Alex spotted a large sack chair in the other corner. "Oh, let me try this one," she said. Alex sank down into the fluffy warmth.

"Oh…" she said. "I think I like this even better."

"Okay, kids," they heard Mrs. Keats calling. "Come and get your snack."

The kids ran over to the rail. Ace hoisted up the basket. "Thanks, Mom."

"Thank you, Mrs. Keats," Alex said.

"Okay, guys. I am going in to unpack some boxes. I'll see you in a little while."

Ace picked up the basket, and they climbed up the ladder into the loft. They grabbed several cookies and started munching. The windows were open. The sun felt warm and was filtered by the canopy of leaves from the trees.

"Hey look, Ace," Alex said. "There's a crow up on that branch. I think it is Corvus."

Ace looked up.

The crow was watching them.

"Alex, did you bring the pendant?" Ace asked.

"Yep, it's right here in my backpack." She pulled it out of the pocket. It was warm in her hand as she handed it to Ace.

"It sure is warm," he said.

Alex nodded.

He held it thoughtfully for a few minutes before handing it back. A flapping of wings startled them both as Corvus landed on a branch close to the open window. He winked at them and then tapped his beak on a knob of a branch three times.

A purple haze grew around the stones in the pendant.

Alex looked at Ace with a smile. Ace grinned. "I think it's go time," he said with a laugh.

The purple haze grew larger, and a door appeared in the middle. Ace pushed his hand on the door handle, and as the door opened up, Ace and Alex felt themselves moving quickly through the tunnel. It felt less scary, Alex thought. She relaxed her body and closed her eyes. Very shortly, they tumbled out on top of the same hill in Aspen Acres.

"Wow," Ace said. "That is starting to feel kind of fun."

Alex laughed. "I know."

Corvus jumped off a branch and landed close to the kids. He looked at them with bright eyes.

"Well, good afternoon, kids. I'm happy to see you."

"Hi, Corvus," Alex said. "We want you to know that we want to help you. We want to help save the magic."

Corvus nodded with approval. "I am happy to hear that," he said with a smile.

"Corvus," Ace asked, "where do we start? How do we reunite the pendant with Maddie?"

"Well, we will start today. First of all, I want you to meet one of my partners, one of my closest friends."

Alex watched as a beautiful red fox came out of the meadow and danced up the hill towards them. Her fur was soft red, and her tail was luxurious and full. Her eyes were blue, and her snout was crisp and narrow. She pranced with a certain elegance as she neared the kids. Corvus looked at her with approval.

Ace muttered, "Whoa," and nudged Alex's arm.

"Hi, Ginger," Corvus said with a smile. "Meet the kids."

The fox came up to Ace and smelled his leg. Then she went over to Alex and sniffed her hand.

"I should really be nervous," Alex whispered to Ace.

"This day keeps getting stranger and stranger," he whispered back.

"My pleasure," Ginger drawled. "I am Ginger Cinnamon Tenderfoot. I'm happy to meet you both."

Corvus explained, "Ginger is my second-in-command. We want to help you as much as we can."

Alex remembered the fox they'd seen while camping. Ginger looked at her with a smile. "Yes, that was me," she said with a laugh. "We were keeping an eye on things."

How did she know I was thinking that? Alex wondered.

Ginger continued. "The Council appreciates your help. We want to start by showing you several scenes so you can learn more about the pendant. Then we are going to take you into town. Maddie is holding a class on healing, and it should be very interesting."

She looked over at Ace. He nodded with a grin, so Alex knew he was ready for this adventure as well.

"Okay, kids," Ginger said, "follow me."

Corvus flew from tree to tree as Ginger led them down the hill and into the meadow, which led to a wooded area. There was a dirt path woven between aspens. Ace went first, and Alex was happy to follow. She felt nervous. The light green color of the leaves was calming, and Alex felt herself relax after several steps. She looked at Ace. "This looks kind of familiar."

Ace nodded. "Yep, it does. It looks like the place Corvus took us yesterday."

The forest opened to a clearing. It was a semi-circle, with a tall rock face in front of them. There was a wooden bench, and Ginger nodded toward it. "You all go ahead and sit down. Make yourselves comfortable."

The kids sat down. Alex was surprised when she saw a hologram appear on the rock face. Ace leaned over and whispered to her, "Wow."

Images started to appear.

There was a figure in the distance. The scene locked into place, and the figure became clear. It was a young woman. She had long red hair, rich with curls, and she was wearing a willowy blue dress that reached below her knees. She looked happy, and as the scene expanded, they could see that she was walking by a stream. A small dog was prancing nearby. The sky was deep rich blue, and there were mountains in the distance. She turned around, smiling. A man approached her. He was also smiling. There was a box in his hand, with a pink ribbon tied around it. He handed it to her. She smiled with delight and opened the box. She pulled out a pendant! It looked like the one Alex and Ace found. They could see the woman's eyes widen, and her smile brightened even more. The man placed the pendant around the woman's neck and gave her a kiss on the cheek. The picture faded away.

Ginger and Corvus watched the kids. "Corvus, is that the pendant? Who were they?" Ace asked.

Corvus responded. "That is the man who made the pendant. He gave it to his wife."

Ginger said, "Here is the next scene."

They were looking at a small log home. Alex thought it looked like the log home that was at the bottom of the hill. There was smoke coming out of the chimney. Snow was falling, and the trees were coated with a thick blanket of snow. It was dark, and the kids could see bright stars dotting the sky. The next image moved them inside the cabin. It was the same woman they'd seen the time before.

Her red hair had long curls tumbling around her shoulders. She was sitting in a rocking chair. There was a fireplace in the corner, stacked with several logs. The dog was lying by the fire, looking at the woman.

The woman was singing softly and holding a bundle in her arms. Alex looked closely. "I think she is holding a baby," she whispered to Ace.

As she said that, the image zoomed into the middle of the hologram, and they could see the baby was sleeping. The front door opened, and a swirl of snow was falling behind the man who walked in. He wiped his feet on a mat. It was the man who had given the woman the pendant. He came over, kneeled down, and gave her and the baby a kiss. He looked peaceful and happy. The couple both looked up and seemed to be looking directly at Alex and Ace, confusion in their eyes. They put their gaze back on the baby, and the vision swirled away.

Corvus hopped next to the kids. Ginger was sitting close by. "That baby is Maddie. She inherits the pendant eventually. She grows up protected by the magic within it." Ginger added, "Rusty's family is becoming aware of the potential magic, though. Here is one more scene to watch."

The kids watched as another living picture came up on the rock. It was a different cabin. There was a man, a woman, and a boy sitting at the kitchen table. The man had a frown on his face. The woman was sitting still, her mouth pinched in a scowl. The man said, "That pendant should be mine. My grandfather made it. He gave it to my brother instead of me. It's not fair." The woman agreed. "Yes, we could use it to make us stronger. That small sapphire he left you gives us some power, but it keeps resisting the energy we put into it. We need more magic so we can overcome that resistance. I want more than this little cabin," she said in a nasty tone. "You promised me. And Rusty needs more stuff. More toys." The boy nodded his head in agreement. The man shook his head. "Don't worry. I have a plan."

With that, the movie faded and swirled away.

28

Alex and Ace looked at each other. Ace said, "So that's why they want the pendant. They want it for themselves, not to help others."

Ginger nodded wisely. "Yes, Ace. That is true. That family got infused with greed. Let's talk more about CAGE. The council was formed when indications of magic started getting stronger. We wanted to make sure that the greatest good was always chosen and that magic didn't go dark."

Corvus added, "But the magic did go dark when the sapphire amulet was infused. The Stone Heart family found that, when they used magic for their own good, they could make things happen in their favor. Rain would fall to nourish their crops, but not rain on their neighbor's land, drying their crops and making them worthless."

Corvus nodded his head at Ginger.

She continued. "The town was concerned, and reasoning with the family did nothing. So, CAGE was formed to correct this event and monitor other ways No-Good magic was spreading. As you saw, Rusty Stone Heart was just a boy when his mom and dad chose the No-Good path."

Ginger shook her head sadly. "It tainted him. The council gathered enough nature magic to neutralize the amulet. It became harmless. However, there is a fifty-year window. If Rusty can find the pendant in the next seven days, he can infuse it with Greed. The pendant has weakened over the years, and Rusty knows enough about magic to influence it to go dark. That is his goal. He is the only one left in his family. The pendant is meant for good. However, if Rusty Stone Heart finds it before we can get it back to its rightful owner, there is the possibility the good magic is weak enough that Rusty could change it to Greed and No-Good."

Alex felt sad that Rusty's family made that choice. She felt even stronger about returning the pendant to Maddie, wherever she was now. "What do you think his plan is?" she asked.

"That is a great question," Ginger answered. "We will likely find clues along the way."

Corvus chirped, "We have one more scene to show you."

Alex was fascinated by how real the images appeared on the rock.

They could see Maddie's cabin. Her mother was sitting on the porch. She had a smile on her face as she watched a toddler play in the yard.

"That's Maddie when she was three," Corvus said.

The dog they saw in the other scenes was running by the child, and she giggled as she started to chase him. The dog stumbled into a small hole and started whimpering as he lifted his leg. He limped and held his back paw up.

Maddie sat next to him with a concerned look on her face. Her mom came over and gently examined his paw. Maddie reached up and grabbed the pendant her mom was wearing. The chain was long enough, and Maddie held it by the dog's paw with a calm expression on her face. Her mom looked at her with surprise. Maddie sat there for several minutes holding the pendant over the paw. Then she let go of the chain and ran off laughing. Her mom watched with a quizzical look, and a small smile began to form. The dog got up and started walking to Maddie. After a few steps, the limp was gone, and the dog started running playfully around her. She leaned down and hugged the dog.

The image slowly swirled and faded away.

Corvus said, "Ginger, let's tell the kids what we are going to do next."

Ginger nodded. She sat up. "You have seen scenes from when Maddie and Rusty were young. Now, in this timeline today, they are young adults. Maddie is a healer. She teaches about herbs. She always wears the pendant because of the energy it has for Good. She doesn't talk about it because it is her sacred tool. She helps those who are interested to find their own tools for healing and health. She is holding a class today that is open to the community. We think you both should go."

Alex said, "That sounds so amazing. I wish my mom were here so she could go, too. She loves that kind of stuff. She is always telling me how powerful we are."

Ginger nodded. "Yes, your mom is a very wise woman. Maybe someday we can bring her here and show her around. But we can't do that yet." Ginger smiled.

Alex felt excited to learn more and to see what Maddie looked like now.

"Maybe it will help us recognize her when we get back to our home," Ace said.

Alex laughed. "We are always thinking the same thing."

"Let's get back to the meadow," Corvus said cheerfully. Ginger led the way down the path. Soon they were close to the hill. "Home base," Alex said to Ace.

Ace smiled.

They looked across the meadow to Maddie's cabin. Alex loved seeing the big pots of flowers and shrubs. It looked so cheerful, she thought.

Ginger and Corvus led them into town through a path in the meadow. The path opened up to a building at the end of a street. There were several adults standing in the yard of the building talking. Several young boys were running close by laughing and chasing each other.

Ginger said, "I'll wait back here. I don't want anyone to see me."

Corvus flew up and landed on the end of a branch. "I'll be just fine up here. I'll be able to keep an eye on things. And we have a few friends in place keeping watch as well. You kids go upstairs and find a seat. We will be waiting for you when it's over."

A lone black cat sat on a fence post watching the building. The cat turned her head and looked at Ace and Alex. The cat nodded to Ginger and Corvus. Ginger smiled and sank back into the meadow grass.

Alex looked at the cat who yawned as they walked by her. Ace nudged Alex. "Do you think she is one of our protectors?"

Alex shook her head. "I have no idea. Let's go see what this is about."

Alex and Ace went up the stairs and entered a large open room. There were wooden chairs set up in rows. Most of them were taken.

There was a young woman at the front of the room. She had long red hair that fell in wide curls around her face. Her eyes were blue and bright, and she had a friendly smile on her face. She was wearing a long yellow dress. The purple pendant was around her neck and looked stunning, Alex thought. But how could the pendant be in two places? She felt the pendant in her jean pocket.

Maddie was talking to a woman who held a toddler in her arms. The toddler was resting his head on the woman's shoulders. Maddie looked at the child with kind eyes and patted him on the back gently.

Alex and Ace found two chairs towards the back of the room close to a window.

Alex looked out the window. Sitting on a branch on a tree not too far away was Corvus. She pointed him out to Alex, who smiled. It made Alex feel good to know Corvus was close by.

The chatter in the room quieted when Maddie started talking. "Hello, everyone! Thank you so much for coming. We are going to have a great discussion today."

Alex leaned in.

"Who here wants a healthier life? One filled with energy, health, and vitality? We are going to talk about ways you can make that happen."

Maddie continued. "We all have a power within us that we can connect to. When we get very quiet, we can hear the messages our bodies are telling us."

That sounds like meditation, Alex thought.

Maddie went on. "Sometimes, there are things in the earth that can help us. It may be an herb, or a flower, or even a stone, or a rock. When we believe it with our heart and feel it in our mind, great things can happen."

Alex noticed that the audience was watching Maddie intently.

The woman and the toddler were sitting a few rows ahead. Alex noticed that the toddler seemed more active. He was sitting on his mom's lap laughing and playing with her hair. The mom smiled and stood up. "I know this to be true. My baby has been suffering with an earache for several days now. It's been so painful for him. After

32

Maddie and I talked yesterday, and then again today, he is so much better. Thank you!" The woman sat down.

Maddie smiled at her. "Your little guy is more powerful than we know," she responded. "You did the right things, had the right thoughts, and also worked with his doctor to give him the best chance to heal. We just helped things along by doing some healing work."

There was a noise that came from the back of the room. A young man with an angry look on his face stood at the door defiantly. "This is all hogwash," he yelled. "Maddie is a fraud. She just wants to take advantage of our town."

Maddie looked at him calmly. "Rusty, please go. We are not going to allow you to ruin this day."

Rusty sneered at her. "Oh yeah? What are you going to do about it? I think it's time people knew the truth."

Alex could feel Ace start to get up. She pushed on his arm and shook her head no. Several men stood up and approached Rusty. Alex whispered, "That man looks familiar." Ace agreed with a nod of his head.

One said, "Son, you can sit here quietly and listen, or better yet just turn around and leave." Both men stood in front of Rusty, blocking his entrance into the room. Rusty looked around in frustration. Then he threw his hands up in the air, turned around, and left.

Maddie gathered her composure. "Okay, where were we?"

She finished her talk, but Alex was distracted, wondering why Rusty was so angry.

Alex and Ace talked quietly as they waited for the room to empty. Maddie was talking to several people who were lined up at the front of the room.

"That was Rusty Stone Heart," Ace said in a quiet voice. "I really wanted to go over there."

"Yes," Alex responded. "He is trying to cause trouble."

The kids walked outside and went towards the meadow. They started down the path knowing Ginger and Corvus would find

33

them. Sure enough, within just a few steps, they could see Ginger smiling and her luxurious tale raise up and swing around her body.

Corvus hopped on a branch close by and looked inquisitive.

"So, you met Rusty," he said. "I saw him coming."

The kids told Ginger and Corvus about the meeting. Alex said, "And I think Maddie helped the little boy feel better. But she didn't say anything like that."

Ginger nodded. "Yes, she doesn't mention the pendant, but it does allow her to amplify healing. It gives her confidence."

Ace said, "I really wanted to get up when he came in."

Corvus replied, "It's good you didn't. We have to keep you two under the radar for a while."

Ace agreed, but Alex could tell he was still frustrated by Rusty's behavior.

"Ginger," Alex asked, "how can the pendant be in two places at once? Maddie had it around her neck, but it was in my pocket."

Ginger explained. "You and Ace are in a different timeline here. You are a part of it, yet because you live in another timeline, things work differently."

"Kids, Rusty may try something else," Corvus said. "But for now, we'd better get you home."

CHAPTER FIVE
Mountain Top Monday

"Two roads diverged in some wood, and I—I took the one less traveled by, and that has made all the difference."
~Robert Frost

The next day was a holiday. It was family and friends' day at Mountain Top Retirement Home, where Mrs. Keats worked. Alex was excited to be going to help. She and Ace had been there several times to volunteer, and she loved talking to the people who lived there.

After breakfast, Alex and her dad drove to Ace's house to pick him up.

The kids chatted on the short drive.

Ace said, "Did you dream up any ideas?"

Alex smiled. "No," she said. "How about you?"

"Nope," Ace responded cheerfully. "But I hope they are grilling hot dogs today.

Ace leaned over and whispered, "And tomorrow we will wait in the treehouse, so Corvus can come get us."

Alex was excited at that thought. She felt happy to be helping, and she wanted to go back to that magical place.

Mr. Emerson pulled up to the main entrance of the retirement home.

It was a square-shaped building with a sprawling outdoor area. Large pine trees dotted the yard, and big pots of colorful flowers greeted them as they walked to the entrance. Mr. Emerson said, "Have fun, kids."

Alex gave her dad a hug.

Mrs. Keats waved from the doorway, smiled, and said, "Hi! Come on in. We are painting birdhouses."

The inside was cozy and comfortable. There was a large living room with big, overstuffed chairs arranged around a fireplace. In one corner, Alex noticed a large table where several older adults were working on a project. Ace said the people who lived here were called residents, since this was their home.

Melissa, the activity director, came up. "Hi, Ace and Alex," she said, with a cheery grin. "We are glad you were able to come today. Do you want to paint a birdhouse? Chuck made them."

"Oh, yes," Alex said. "This will be fun."

Melissa walked with them.

"Hi, Chuck," Ace said. Chuck was sitting in a wheelchair at the other end of the table and smiled at the kids. He was painting the trim with a bright blue.

"Good morning, young man," Chuck said, with a booming voice. "And good morning to you, too, Alex."

"These are so pretty, Chuck," she said. There were various sizes. "I bet the birds will love these."

Alex wondered if Corvus had a birdhouse, and if he did, what it looked like.

Miss Jenny was sitting next to him, intent on what she was painting. Miss Lillian was at the other end sitting next to a young girl. She was whispering to her and noticed the kids. She had a big smile. "Come down here, kids! Do you know Annabelle? This is Melissa's daughter."

Alex liked Miss Lillian. She always had a smile on her face, and she was fun to talk to.

"Hi, Annabelle," Alex said.

"Hi," the little girl said, a bit shyly.

Alex sat next to Miss Lillian, and Ace sat next to Annabelle. The morning passed quickly. Alex painted her birdhouse bright yellow. She added small pink flowers to the front. Miss Lillian said, "Annabelle starts first grade this year. She told me she's a little nervous."

Alex leaned over. "Oh, you will love first grade! You will learn so much."

"Yes," Ace added, "and you get to go out and play twice each day."

Annabelle smiled at the thought of that.

After they were finished, Melissa came over. "Why don't you kids go out and play until lunch?"

Alex looked at Annabelle. "Do you want to come with us?" she asked. Annabelle looked at her mom, who nodded her head.

The kids went outside. The sun was warm, and the temperature, pleasant. The yard sprawled out for quite a distance. There were tall ponderosa pines, red maples, and purple ash trees offering plenty of shade.

Melissa gave them a ball, and the three of them ran around the back yard kicking it and laughing. Some of the residents were sitting out in a shaded area close to some picnic tables. Josh, the chef, was at the grill, and Alex could smell the hamburgers cooking. Alex felt very happy. Annabelle came running over to her.

"Catch!" she called, throwing the ball to Alex. As Alex ran over to catch it, Annabelle stumbled over a branch on the ground and fell. The little girl sat up and started to cry. Alex ran over to her. Annabelle's knee was skinned and bleeding. Ace saw what happened and ran over, too.

"I'm so sorry, honey," Alex said. "Let me take a look." Alex leaned over Annabelle's leg.

She could feel the pendant in her shirt become very warm. Alex remembered the scene where Maddie held the pendant close to the dog's sore foot. She decided to lean against the little girl's leg so the warmth of the pendant would be close to the injury.

Annabelle sobbed, "I'm okay. I'm okay. But I want my mom." Melissa came out and saw Annabelle sitting and ran over.

Alex kept the pendant close until Melissa came. She said, "Oh my goodness. Look at the scrape. Let's get you inside and cleaned up."

Annabelle got up, and they walked with her to the door to the patio. Melissa turned with a smile. "It's okay, kids! We will be back soon. Why don't you go join the others?"

Alex felt badly that Annabelle had fallen and gotten such a large scrape. "I hope she's okay," she said.

Ace replied, "I think she'll be fine."

Alex told him how the pendant felt so warm and how she was able to keep it close to the injury. "Maybe it will help," Ace said. "We will see."

Josh hollered, "Come on, let's eat!"

Alex and Ace helped serve the residents and then filled their own plates. They sat next to Miss Lillian and Chuck, who were cousins.

Miss Lillian said, "Remember how we used to climb trees and watch the birds?"

Chuck replied, "I sure do. You always climbed higher and faster than me."

Miss Lillian laughed.

Annabelle came out and sat by Ace. Alex said gently, "How are you feeling? I'm so sorry you fell playing with me."

Annabelle said, "It feels good!" She smiled and dug into her food.

Dessert was homemade cookies and ice cream. Alex made sure Annabelle got her ice cream first. Annabelle had a big smile as she took a bite out of the cone.

Mr. Keats came in just as everyone was finishing eating. "Well, it looks like everyone had a great time! Kids, are you ready to go? Alex is going to stay with us until her parents get home from work."

Ace and Alex said goodbye. They also stopped to say goodbye to Mrs. Keats. As they were going out the front door, Annabelle ran up. "Alex, look! The scrape is gone!"

Alex and Ace looked at the little girl's knee. Sure enough, the open scrape had closed almost all the way.

Alex gave her a hug. "Oh, I am so glad!" she said.

Alex and Ace looked at each other. In the car, Ace whispered, "Do you think the pendant helped?"

Alex answered, "I think so."

Chapter Six

Tuesday Trouble

*"Don't let what you can't do stop you
from doing what you can do."*
~John Wooden

The next morning, Alex and her dad rode their bikes to Ace's house. Rocky ran alongside. Alex was happy she was going to spend the day with Ace and his dad. Ace was on his bike when they arrived.

"Hi," he said cheerfully. "Do you want to go ride up the hill?"

Alex looked at her dad, who nodded his head. "Take Rocky with you, and stay on the bike path."

Alex gave her dad a hug. Mr. Emerson was standing on the porch sipping on a cup of coffee. "Have fun, kids. Let me know when you get back. I'll be in my office."

The dads chatted while the kids waved goodbye.

They rode up the sidewalk to the top of the hill. Alex pushed hard on the pedals to keep moving forward. At the top, there was a bench with a beautiful view of downtown Aspen Acres and the mountains to the west. She felt content as she sipped on water and caught her breath.

Ace said, "That hill is tough, but it is so pretty up here."

Alex agreed. She poured some water into a collapsible dog dish she carried in her knapsack. Rocky lapped it up and looked at her with thankful eyes, then he curled up by her feet.

Alex said, "How do we find Maddie? Should we put an ad in the paper?"

Ace shrugged his shoulders. "I don't know. It's hard when we don't even know where she is."

Alex was thoughtful. "Ginger and Corvus are telling us to be aware and watch for clues. I'm just not sure."

Ace agreed. "I know. The next time we go back to the old Aspen Acres, let's be very aware. Maybe there is something we are not seeing."

Rocky raised his head and looked at him. He seemed to smile before he laid his head down and went back to sleep.

Alex giggled. "Rocky is so funny."

Ace said, "He's the best. I can't wait to get my dog. My mom and dad said maybe in a few months, after we get settled."

Alex said, "That's great. I bet your dog and Rocky will become great friends, too."

The kids sat for a while looking at the views and enjoying the warm sun and soft breeze.

"Well, the way down will be much easier," Ace said. "Let's head back and have lunch."

Alex enjoyed the ride down the hill. She didn't need to use her pedals but kept a careful touch on the brakes when she felt like she was going too fast.

After lunch, Alex and Ace climbed up to the loft. They looked out the window, but they could not see Corvus.

"I wonder if he is going to come get us today," Alex said.

"I don't know," Ace said. "I hope so. We need more clues because we only have a few days left."

Alex pulled the pendant out of her pocket, and they both held it. The pendant became warm, but no haze appeared.

Alex said, "Corvus, are you out there? We want to talk to you."

Ace looked out on the branch close to the window.

"I don't see him," he said.

They heard something scurrying up the branch. A small squirrel was climbing up the tree and came out on the branch. It was an

Abert's squirrel with the little tuft of hair on the top of his head. The squirrel peered into the window with tiny brown eyes. He backed away and pushed three times against the knob in the tree that Corvus used.

Alex and Ace looked at each other. As they watched, the purple haze grew around the pendant, and the door appeared.

"I guess he is going to help us," Alex said. "Maybe Corvus is busy."

Ace said, "Let's go." He grabbed Alex's hand and pushed the door in his other hand. Off they went, down the invisible slippery slide tumbling out on top of the hill.

Alex and Ace were met on the hill by Ginger. Her tail swept behind her and over her back, and she sat on her haunches. She looked worried. "Kids," she said, "we need your help. Rusty is up to no good. Corvus just got a bark alert from Rusty's dog, and he is in communication with CAGE right now."

"What's going on?" Alex asked.

They looked at the cabin as Maddie came out her front door. She carefully locked the door. A car pulled into the driveway. Maddie got into the passenger seat, and they drove away.

Ace said, "I wonder what Rusty is up to now."

Alex nodded. "We want to help."

"Let's head that way, kids," Ginger said.

The three walked down the hill and through the path in the meadow. Ginger cautioned them to stop. They moved closer to several aspen trees, where they could not be seen.

"Maddie is going out of town for the day," Ginger said. "But look."

Down the road, they could see a man riding a bicycle. It was Rusty. He got off his bike at the end of Maddie's driveway and laid it down on the side out of view. He walked towards Maddie's house.

Rusty looked around and went up to the front door. He tried the handle. He went over to the window and pushed up on it. The window was locked.

Alex heard a noise coming from a tree. Corvus flew in and landed close by.

"Well hello, kids. We are so glad you could come today. Rusty is trying to break in to steal the pendant. Maddie had to go away, and, according to our sources, she locked the pendant up, but she left her bedroom window open. Rusty does not know that, but we need to stop him from finding that open window. We need to provide a distraction in order to scare Rusty off."

Corvus nodded his head. There was a black cat sitting on Maddie's porch, seemingly uninterested in doing anything about Rusty's presence, but still watching him intently with her green eyes.

Corvus smiled. "I think we are going to create an event and shoo him away. C'mon kids, let's get you in place before he gets to the bedroom window."

They walked quietly through the aspen grove towards the back of the house. There was a tall tree full of leaves and several low branches.

"Stay here, kids," Corvus whispered. "We want you two to take some rocks and aim for the roof of the house. Maddie has a tin roof, and the noise from the rocks might be enough. We cannot throw as well as you both can."

Alex looked up. The bark covering the middle of the tree started to move and re-arranged into a smile as the top of the tree bent over, offering a sturdy limb. Corvus said, "Go ahead and jump on. There is another branch to hold on to."

Ace and Alex smiled at each other as the large branch slowly rose up to the height of the roof. There was a canopy of leaves and a nest filled with small stones within easy reach.

Ace whispered, "This is so cool. I love this tree."

Alex agreed. There was enough of an opening between the branches that they were able to start throwing the rocks up on the roof.

Rusty stopped for a moment. He was still at the front of the house. He shook his head, but they could see he was wondering

44

where the noise was coming from. He tried another window. Alex and Ace kept throwing stones. Alex looked up at the sky.

"Look," she whispered to Ace. Ace looked up. There was a dark swath of movement shaped like a V, flying quickly towards the house.

Corvus let out a loud caw and flew over Rusty's head. Rusty looked up, an annoyed look on his face. The flock of birds came closer and started to dive towards Maddie's house.

Rusty looked alarmed at all the birds. "This is crazy," he said out loud.

The black cat opened her mouth and yawned. She looked over at where the kids remained hidden in the trees and winked. Alex saw it, too, and smiled.

The birds were geese. They could hear a loud honking sound. The flock quickly formed a pattern of diving down towards Rusty's head and then flying away.

Alex and Ace giggled quietly.

Rusty looked over at the cat, who was now sitting on the porch rail watching the birds fly back and forth. The cat looked at him and yawned again.

Rusty threw his hands up in anger.

"This place is crazy. I'm outta here." He walked down the driveway to his bike and pulled it out of the weeds. He looked back at the house, where the birds continued to fly in streaks and he could still hear the noise of the stones hitting the tin roof. He shook his head in disgust and rode away.

Corvus was happy.

"You did it!" he said. "Thank you, crew!"

He flew over to the flock and said a few words. The kids could not hear what he said, but it looked like everyone was happy. The geese, honking and baying like a pack of hound dogs, flew off across the horizon.

The tree bent over, and the branch lowered gently to the ground. The kids jumped off.

"He won't be back," Ginger drawled. "That was enough to scare him off for a while. Tabby will keep watch until Maddie gets home. Good job, Tabby," Ginger said.

Tabby winked again, laid back down on the porch, and closed her eyes.

Alex looked back at the tree now standing tall and stately.

They walked back up the hill.

Alex said, "The pendant does heal." She explained the story to Corvus and Ginger. "It helped Annabelle when she fell!"

Ace added, "She hardly had a mark on her knee a few hours later."

"Nicely done," Corvus said proudly.

Ginger said, "The pendant is still powerful. I'm glad you were able to help Annabelle."

Corvus said, "Kids, thank you for your help today. Any progress finding Maddie on your end?"

He was matter of fact. "We only have a few days left."

Alex shook her head. "No. We're not even sure where to start. How do we find her?"

Ace added, "Can we put an ad in the paper? In our neighborhood online community? We can't ask our parents for help, so we are not sure what to do next." Ace sounded discouraged.

"Remember, kids, all the clues are there. It will happen." Ginger added, "Think about this quote. 'Don't let what you can't do stop you from doing what you can do.' John Wooden said that. He was a famous basketball player and coach. You kids are doing great. Just be on the lookout for signs of magic. They are there."

CHAPTER SEVEN

Wednesday Worries

"Try to be a rainbow in someone else's cloud."
~ Maya Angelou

Alex's mom dropped her off at the front entrance of Mountain Top Retirement Home. Ace was sitting in a rocking chair. His mom was at the door and waved at Alex and her mom with a big smile.

"See you later, honey," Mrs. Emerson said.

"Okay, Mom, have a great day," Alex said, as she bounded out of the car.

Ace came up to greet her. "Hi, Alex. I've been helping Chuck in the workshop. We are building more birdhouses."

"Cool," Alex said. "I want to help, too."

The children walked into the main living area. The bustle of breakfast was over. Alex saw Miss Lillian sitting by the window reading the paper. "Let me go say hi," she said to Ace.

"Okay," Ace said cheerfully. "Come meet us in the workshop when you're done."

Alex nodded and walked over to Miss Lillian. "Good morning!"

Miss Lillian looked up, and her eyes brightened. "Well hello, dear. It's so nice to see you. Come sit next to me."

Alex enjoyed talking to Miss Lillian. She was kind and thoughtful and knew just what to say.

47

"How are you?" Miss Lillian asked. "Tell me about your summer so far. We have not had a chance to talk about important stuff in a while."

Alex told her about the camping trip and how much fun they'd had. She wanted to tell her about finding the pendant and their assignment to find the owner, but she knew that she couldn't.

Miss Lillian's eyes brightened again. "Oh, how I miss camping," she said. "It was one of my favorite things to do as a child. Sometimes, Chuck and my aunt and uncle would come along. We had so much fun." Miss Lillian sighed. "Those memories mean so much to me."

She leaned over and looked at Alex. "You never know what you might find in these Colorado mountains."

Alex smiled back. *That's for sure*, she thought to herself.

They sat in silence for a few minutes. There were birdhouses outside the window. Alex enjoyed watching the small birds pecking at the seeds and flying from branch to branch. It felt peaceful.

Miss Lillian patted her hand. "I think I am going to go back to my room and rest for a while," she said. "I feel quite tired today."

She looked pale, Alex thought. "I'm happy to push your wheelchair back for you," she offered.

"That would be wonderful, my dear," Miss Lillian responded.

She brought Miss Lillian to her room. Alex noticed a small bird print on her dresser, much like the one Ace had in his treehouse. She pointed at it, and Miss Lillian nodded with a smile. "Oh yes, my dear, I'll tell you the story about that bird someday." As Miss Lillian got out of her wheelchair to lie down on her bed, she said, "You know, one of my favorite poets is Maya Angelou. She said, 'Try to be a rainbow in someone else's cloud.' That's you, my dear. You'd better go check on those boys now, and make sure they are staying out of mischief!"

Miss Lillian closed her eyes. Alex smiled as she left the room. Once again, Miss Lillian knew just what to say.

The workshop was a bevy of activity. Chuck and Ace were in one corner. Chuck was holding a piece of pine steady while Ace gently hammered several nails. Chuck looked over. "C'mon over, Alex!"

he called. "This young man is doing well. Let's get you started. We are starting to assemble this one."

Alex looked at the small pile of wood pieces and nails. She liked the smell of the wood. She added wood glue to the sides as they got ready to attach the roof. Chuck hammered the last few nails and added the wooden perch. With a smile, he held it up.

"Excellent work, kids. Let's go have lunch. This one will be ready to hang outside." He added it to a table that held four completely assembled birdhouses.

The kids walked with Chuck to the dining room. Alex said, "I wonder if Miss Lillian is feeling better. She wasn't feeling good earlier and wanted to rest."

Miss Lillian was not in the dining area. Chuck said, "You kids go ahead and get lunch. I'll go check on her."

Alex and Ace sat at a table by the window. Chuck soon returned. "She said she'll eat in her room. She's still not feeling well." Chuck had a concerned look on his face for a moment. "I'm sure she will feel better soon. I'll check back later."

After lunch, Chuck said. "Let's go hang those birdhouses."

Alex and Ace carried them outside to a table. Chuck was supervising one of the maintenance men, Tommy, who had a ladder set up by a tree.

"Yep," he said, "that's the perfect branch." Tommy smiled as he climbed several steps on the ladder and carefully hung the birdhouse on a knob in the tree. Soon, the back grounds were dotted with birdhouses attached to several trees.

Chuck looked proud. "The birds around here will have good shelter this fall and winter. Thank you, Tommy, and thank you, Ace and Alex."

Tommy smiled as he folded up his ladder. "Happy to help," he said.

Alex felt happy. Ace said, "Let's go check on Miss Lillian. Mom said my dad will be here soon to pick us up, Alex. We can hang out in the treehouse until you have to go home."

Chuck's face brightened. "Oh, a treehouse. I bet that is a fun place to be. Maybe we should build another birdhouse for your treehouse." Chuck laughed.

Alex thought that was a great idea. "Yes, she said. "That will be fun."

Miss Lillian's door was shut. A nurse came out. "Hi kids, she is sleeping right now."

"Okay," said Ace. "We will check on her tomorrow."

The nurse responded, "Sounds good. Don't worry. We will take good care of her."

Alex felt nervous in her stomach. She said to Ace, "I wish there was more we could do."

Ace responded, "Well, I bet she will be better tomorrow."

Chapter Eight

Thursday Triumph

"Into each life, some rain must fall."
~ Henry Wadsworth Longfellow

The next morning, Alex was sitting in Ace's kitchen. Mr. Keats put a plate of pancakes in front of her. "Here you go, Alex," he said with a smile. "Eat up." Ace handed her a bottle of maple syrup.

Mrs. Keats came in. "Kids, I called to get an update on Miss Lillian. She is still not feeling well. The doctor was in last night. We think it would be better for you guys to stay here today instead of going to the home just in case anyone else gets sick."

Alex was disappointed. Mr. Keats noticed the look on her face. "Don't worry too much," he said gently. "They will take good care of her, and I'll be glad for the company today. I'm glad you brought Rocky today, too."

Rocky was lying in the corner of the kitchen but sat up and looked at Mr. Keats when he heard his name. He came over to him and sat patiently, waiting for a treat.

That made the kids giggle, and Mr. Keats offered a dog biscuit, which Rocky eagerly accepted.

After Mrs. Keats left for work, the kids sat on the ground by the treehouse. Alex was glum. Ace had his head in his hands. Rocky was lying close by with his head in Alex's lap. He looked sad, too, Alex thought.

51

"I'm not sure what we are supposed to do next," Ace said. "We are running out of time."

"I know," Alex said. She pulled the pendant out of her pocket. It was warm.

"Feel it," she said, as she handed it to Ace.

"Yep, it sure is warm," he responded.

It was a warm day. The sun was bright, and several wispy clouds floated across the sky. The kids sat for a few minutes, holding the pendant. "I wish we could go to old Aspen Acres right now and talk to Corvus and Ginger," Ace said.

Alex looked up at the tree, but there was no sign of Corvus or their squirrel friend.

Ace was looking at the pendant. "I wonder what will happen if we could open the latch on the side?"

He tried to push it, but the latch did not move.

"I know," Alex said. "I've never been able to get it open either."

She pushed on the latch, too. It was stuck. Alex felt frustrated and took a deep breath.

"Ace, let's try something. Let's take some deep breaths and think about how wonderful it would be to go to Aspen Acres today. Let's not struggle anymore."

"Can't hurt," Ace responded.

Alex and Ace sat side by side. With each deep breath, Alex started to relax.

After a few minutes, Ace said, "I feel better, too. I know we can figure it out."

The pendant was on the ground between them. Ace picked it up and pushed on the latch. It opened easily and, as it did, the purple haze appeared from the middle. Alex was delighted and her eyes brightened. She said, "Look! It's starting."

Rocky looked up and whined quietly. Ace gently grabbed Rocky's collar. "C'mon, boy, you can come with us. Let's do this."

With confidence and ease, Alex and Ace pushed against the ethereal door and stepped in. Like always, the kids felt pulled forward. Alex felt Rocky by her side, and she was able to relax as she moved down the inner slide. After a few minutes, she toppled out. She looked over at Ace, who was standing next to her. Rocky jumped out of the haze and started running around the hill in circles.

"Never stops being cool," Ace said with a smile. The kids looked around.

The weather in old Aspen Acres was much different. The sun was gone, and the sky was dark and threatening. Over the mountains, they could hear a crack of thunder as a lightning bolt blazed across the sky. "Wow, what happened here?" Ace wondered.

Alex looked around and saw a bird flying towards them. It was Corvus. He landed on a branch and looked down at them. He was out of breath. "Kids, I didn't come get you! I did not want you to come because the weather is so bad." He looked at Rocky. "And you brought Rocky? Oh no, I don't think this is good at all."

Alex had never seen Corvus so upset. Rocky looked up and barked once. Then he said, "No problem, Corvus. I'm here to help my kids."

Rocky sat up straight and looked Corvus in the eye.

Alex smiled. "Rocky, you can talk!"

Ace said, "Rocky, we are so glad you are here with us!"

Rocky wagged his tail. "Well, it's about time I got invited to see what's been going on. I've been able to do nothing on the other side but chase squirrels."

Corvus shrugged his shoulders. "Your power is growing," he said. "You were able to get here by yourselves. But I don't think you should stay right now."

They looked and saw Ginger run out of the meadow and up the hill towards them. She said urgently, "We have a big problem. Maddie is on her way to help a neighbor who fell ill. She is walking by the river, and we just got a Bark Alert that Rusty left his house and is heading that way. The rain we had earlier is making the river rise, and it's about to rain again." Ginger shook her snout side to side. "We need to do something, Corvus." She went over and sniffed Rocky. "Well, big fella, I guess you are going to help us, too."

Rocky lifted a paw and smiled. "My pleasure, I'm sure," he responded politely.

Alex said, "We are in. We want to help, too."

Corvus was reluctant. "Well, okay," he said. "But you need to stick close. And we don't have much time. We need to get you out of here within an hour because storms can mess up timeline travel."

Alex and Ace looked at each other. "If we can help, we want to," Ace said bravely.

They headed down the meadow and walked on a path towards the river. The wind picked up, and it started to rain. They were somewhat protected by the cover of the trees. Alex was startled by a loud clap of thunder. Ace grabbed her hand. Streaks of lightning crisscrossed the sky.

Corvus called to them. "Kids, there's Maddie."

The kids could see her in the distance.

Maddie pulled her scarf tight around her shoulders. She had a knapsack she held closely against her chest. The wind was in her face, and Alex could tell she was having trouble walking against the storm. Suddenly, Rusty appeared right before her. He had a sneer on his face.

"Well, Maddie," he said, "there's no one to protect you here. I want the pendant. It was supposed to be my family's. Not yours. I know you have it. I want it now."

He pushed her.

Maddie stood strong. "Rusty, leave me alone," she said angrily. "Go away. Your family used their magic for Greed and No Good. You know that. You had a choice to do better, and you did not. I am not giving you the pendant."

Rusty pushed her again and, as she lost her balance, the knapsack flew off her chest and fell into the river. It was caught by the current and moved rapidly downstream.

Maddie looked at him and pushed him back. She ran down by the river following the knapsack. She stepped into the water around a bend as the knapsack got caught on a limb. As she made her way towards it, a wall of water rushed down the stream. Maddie lost her balance and yelled for help as she was swept down the river. Rusty looked at her, and then turned and walked away.

Suddenly, Corvus flew up into the storm with a large branch in his mouth. He dropped it over Maddie's head. She did not see where it had come from, but she grabbed it. It was strong enough that she was able to use it to push herself to the edge of the river as Corvus helped guide it. She crawled out, mud caked on her face and hair. She sat on the riverbank with her head in her hands crying.

Meanwhile, Alex watched the river rise. The knapsack had loosened from the limb and was out of sight. Maddie was several hundred yards downstream.

Alex shouted to Ace against the wind. "It has to be here somewhere. I bet the pendant is in it."

Ace agreed. "We have to stop the water somehow so we can go in and find it."

Suddenly the kids heard a loud chatter. They looked in amazement as hundreds of beavers started jumping in the water, one right after the other from both sides of the riverbank. They were chattering back and forth. Ginger looked pleased. Rocky was surprised. "Why, I never…" he said. The beavers had thick fur and webbed feet. Their scale-covered tails were bumping up against each other as the large colony entered the water. Trees by the river fell as the beavers chewed through the woods.

Alex and Ace watched. Within moments, the beavers had created a dam. The rain slowed. The beavers looked at Corvus and Ginger and the kids with big, toothy smiles.

"That should help a bit," one said proudly. Then, just as fast as they had appeared, the beavers turned with a quick salute to Corvus and went over the riverbank and disappeared.

Ginger said, "They are the best."

Ace said, "Let's go find that knapsack."

Alex was already in the water, which was just under her knees. She stepped carefully, as the water was cold, and she did not want to fall in.

"Kids," Corvus urged. "We have to leave very soon."

Alex and Ace started to rummage in the murky water. Alex's heart was beating fast. Ginger was walking close to the shore. "Corvus," she said nervously, "we have to get the kids out of here, now!"

Rocky was sitting by the edge of the water watching Alex. He jumped in and started paddling to her. He sniffed. "Here," he said, "try here." Alex moved her hand deep in the water.

Suddenly, Alex felt a cloth bag jammed up against a rock. "Ace!" she yelled.

Ace splashed over to her. Together, they tugged on the bag. The water had calmed but was still swirling around them. They tugged and pulled against the current. Finally, the bag released from the rock. It was the knapsack!

The kids carried it to the riverbank. Alex could feel the edge of the pendant within the bag. Rocky swam to the shore and was shaking himself off as he walked up the bank.

"We have to give this back to Maddie," Ace said urgently.

"We are running out of time," Corvus said, with a worried look. The kids ran towards Maddie. Ginger, Corvus, and Rocky were right behind them. Maddie was walking towards them with her head down. They could see she was still crying. They ran closer.

"Maddie," Ace yelled. "Here! Here is your knapsack. Your pendant is in it!"

Maddie looked up, startled.

Alex pushed it into her hands and smiled. Ace patted her shoulder. "It's okay now," he said gently.

Maddie looked at them with bright eyes and a faint smile.

Corvus yelled, "Now! Before it's too late." The kids looked at Maddie with big grins and then ran quickly to Corvus and Ginger. Rocky was panting as Alex grabbed his collar.

Alex said, "The pendant is not in my pocket anymore."

"No," Corvus said gently. "You have reunited it with its rightful owner. But the door back home is open for just a few more minutes. Please hurry."

Alex watched as the purple haze rose up before them.

"Go now," Corvus said kindly. "We will never forget you or how you helped."

Ginger nodded in agreement. She had a tear in her eye.

Alex felt sudden sadness. She realized they may never see their friends again.

Corvus called out, "And Ace, your aunt was a lovely person. I'm sorry we didn't get to talk about her. Now, go, kids, go."

Ace grabbed her hand and Rocky's collar and then pushed the door. It stuck for a few seconds. Alex pushed it, too, and then they and Rocky swirled down the time slide and fell out on the deck of the treehouse.

Alex looked at Rocky. His fur was wet. He came over and licked her on the face and did the same to Ace. Then he shook himself off, went over to the tree, circled around several times, and closed his eyes. He started to snore softly.

Ace and Alex looked at each other, laughing. They both had wet hair and mud on their shoes.

Alex marveled. "We were never supposed to get the pendant back here," she said. "We were meant to get the pendant back to Maddie back then."

She felt in her pocket again, and, sure enough, the pendant was gone. They sat down on the deck taking in all the events that had happened.

"Ace, I don't think we will ever see Corvus or Ginger again," she said sadly.

"Don't be sad, Alex," Ace replied. "You never know what might happen. And Corvus did know my aunt," he said with wonder. "I wish we knew more about that."

He hugged his friend. "But we saved the pendant from Rusty! We saved the magic!"

"Yes," Alex said, with a hint of a smile. It made her feel better to think about that.

CHAPTER NINE

Friday Finish

"A thing of beauty is a joy forever."
~ John Keats

The next morning, Alex and Ace walked through the front door of Mountain Top Retirement Home. Chuck was sitting in the living room talking to Miss Lillian. She waved them over with a big smile. Alex ran over.

"Miss Lillian, are you feeling better?" she asked, hopefully.

"Oh yes, much better." Miss Lillian smiled. "I was telling Chuck, I had the strangest dream last night. I was in a big storm." She shivered. "There was thunder and lightning. It reminded me of a very scary day when I was young. But then I woke up. And just like that, I was feeling so much better."

"Miss Longfellow, we were worried about you," Chuck said fondly. I can't have anything happen to my favorite cousin, little Maddie." He tousled her hair.

Miss Lillian smiled at Chuck. "Oh my goodness, you know I don't go by that name anymore."

Alex and Ace looked at each other with wide eyes.

"Miss Maddie?" Alex said.

Ace said, "I think we'd better talk, if you feel up to it."

"Of course." Miss Lillian looked at the kids with curiosity.

Chuck said, "Let's go outside. I think I sense a story coming!"

Alex felt awe. So many parts were tumbling into place. She grabbed Ace's hand and squeezed it. Ace returned the pressure. "I can't believe it," he whispered to Alex.

They sat outside on the far end of the patio.

Alex said, "I'm not even sure where to start. But I think it's okay to tell you now."

Ace nodded in agreement. She continued. "It all started when Ace and I went camping a few weeks ago."

Chuck and Miss Lillian were listening intently.

"When we heard Chuck call you Maddie, well, we needed to tell you," Ace added.

Alex took a deep breath. Ace grabbed her arm and pointed. There was a black bird flying towards them.

Miss Lillian and Chuck looked up and saw it, too. The bird flew overhead, and he had something glistening in his beak.

Alex mouthed, "Corvus?" to Ace.

He whispered back, "I think so."

The bird hovered for a few seconds several feet above Miss Lillian's head and dropped a shiny object in her lap. She looked down as she saw her pendant. She picked it up gently and looked at Chuck and the kids with astonishment.

"My pendant?" she said with wonder. Tears formed and started to fall gently down her face.

Chuck wiped his eyes and asked, "Alex, Ace...how did this happen?"

Corvus was sitting on a nearby branch watching them.

Miss Lillian said, "I did go by Maddie when I was younger. Then something happened that changed my life, and I decided it was time to use my middle name, which is Lillian."

She looked at them. "I can't believe this," she said.

Alex took a deep breath, wondering how Miss Lillian and Chuck would react to what she was going to tell them. "We went back in time. We saw Aspen Acres like it was when you were young. It was so cool."

Chuck and Miss Lillian looked at each other with a smile. Chuck leaned in and said, "I told you it would all work out."

Miss Lillian's eyes glistened. "If you see the crow, you must go," she whispered.

Alex looked at her with a smile. "The print in your room," Ace said. "I have one, too."

Miss Lillian nodded. "Now, children, start at the beginning and tell us everything. Please."

Alex and Ace explained all the events that had happened.

Chuck nodded his head when the kids told them that they had been at the class Miss Maddie was teaching. "Yes," he said. "I was one of the men who made sure Rusty left. We were going to have none of that."

Miss Lillian was spellbound. Alex told them how they worked with Corvus, Ginger, and Tabby the day Maddie went away from her house and had the window open in her bedroom.

"And you kids created the distraction so Rusty could not steal the pendant," she said in amazement. "During the flood, I thought it was lost forever. My life became very different. I felt like the magic was gone. I was discouraged for years. I changed my name and left Aspen Acres. I stopped my healing work."

"And," she said with appreciation, "here it is again."

Miss Lillian kept shaking her head. "My pendant. My beautiful pendant." Tears kept streaming down her cheeks. Alex felt happy and relieved and knew the tears were happy ones.

Mrs. Keats come out of the patio door. "C'mon in now," she called. "Time for lunch." Mrs. Keats came out to help Chuck and Miss Lillian inside in their wheelchairs.

"You have a special boy," Chuck said, with a catch in his voice. "And this young lady is quite wonderful as well."

Mrs. Keats looked at them with friendly curiosity. "Well, I could not agree more," she said.

"We will talk more soon. I can't thank you enough," Miss Lillian said, as she hugged Alex and Ace.

"Thank you," Chuck said sincerely.

"We'll be right in, Mom," Ace said.

Ace and Alex sat back in their chairs as Mrs. Keats, Miss Lillian, and Chuck went inside.

"It all makes sense," Ace said. "We were able to get the pendant back to Maddie back then, and now Miss Lillian is better, and we saved the magic."

He looked proud. "High five!" Alex slapped his hand with gusto.

Ace waved at Corvus, who raised his foot and bowed down slightly.

Corvus flew off the branch and towards the kids. He dropped two envelopes, which landed perfectly in their hands. He winked and flew off.

Each envelope had their name written on the front in beautiful script. Alex turned it over. It was embossed with a gold bird foot seal.

"Let's open it," Alex said excitedly.

The kids opened their envelope carefully. Each pulled out a card.

"The Council of All Good Everywhere (CAGE) thanks you for your service. You finished your mission ahead of schedule, and we are so grateful," she read.

"Magic has been restored. We are pleased to grant you a lifetime membership to CAGE.

P.S. Rusty's power is gone, and Maddie's healing powers are being restored, minute by minute.

We are always here if you need us, and we will see you again soon."

It was signed by Corvus, Ginger, and the Council.

Alex and Ace smiled at each other. "I'm so happy we could help," Ace said.

Alex felt proud. "And we will get to see Corvus and Ginger again! I can't wait," she said with a smile.

The kids put the cards carefully back in the envelopes and ran back to the dining room laughing, hand-in-hand. They knew that more adventures were soon to come.

The End (for now).

CPSIA information can be obtained
at www.ICGtesting.com
Printed in the USA
LVHW041136241121
704321LV00004B/290

9 780578 968216